Treasures Unknown.

Once Garth and A.J. had left, I told Og, "We've got a big day tomorrow, too."

This time, Og was silent.

Maybe he wished the treasure was in his tank instead of my cage.

I wanted to open the treasure to see what was inside, but I'd promised Garth I wouldn't peek. It's always a good idea to keep a promise.

Look for all of

HUMPHREY'S TINY TALES

Humphrey's

Treasure Hunt Trouble

Humphrey's
Treasure Hunt Trouble

Betty G. Birney

illustrated by **Priscilla Burris**

PUFFIN BOOKS

PUFFIN BOOKS
An imprint of Penguin Random House LLC
375 Hudson Street
New York, New York 10014

Published simultaneously in the United States of America by G. P. Putnam's Sons
and Puffin Books, imprints of Penguin Random House LLC, 2017

Text copyright © 2017 by Betty G. Birney.
Illustrations copyright © 2017 by Priscilla Burris.

Library of Congress Cataloging-in-Publication Data is available upon request.

Puffin Books ISBN 9780147514622

Printed in the United States of America.

5th Printing

Design by Ryan Thomann and Eileen Savage.

To Anne White, because
good friends are a real treasure
—*B.B.*

For my treasured siblings—
Abi, Becki, Ruthi, Abel and Debbie
—*P.B.*

Humphrey's

Treasure Hunt Trouble

Contents

Secret Treasure

"Can you keep a secret, Humphrey?" Garth whispered.

"Of course," I whispered back. But since I'm a hamster and Garth is a human, all he heard was,

"Squeak!"

"How about you, Og?" Garth
asked my friend.

Og answered, "BOING!" He is

a frog who makes a VERY-VERY-VERY strange sound.

"There's going to be a treasure hunt in my backyard tomorrow," Garth said. "Don't tell anybody, okay?"

"Wow!" I squeaked. I wasn't sure what a treasure hunt was, but it sounded exciting.

"BOING-BOING!" Og splashed around in his tank.

"I've worked out some of the clues already," Garth said. "And I haven't even told A.J."

A.J. is Garth's best friend. They

are both in my class at Longfellow School.

I'm the classroom hamster in Room 26. Og is the classroom frog.

It's part of my job to go home with a different student each weekend, but Og usually stays in Room 26.

This weekend, Garth invited everyone in our class to a party. He even invited Og and me. Our teacher, Mrs. Brisbane, said we could both go. That made me HAPPY-HAPPY-HAPPY.

My cage and Og's tank sat
on the desk in Garth's room.
We watched as he cut paper into
squares.

"The clues should be hard," he said. "But not too hard. After all, somebody has to find the treasure."

"What's the treasure?" I asked, wishing Garth could understand me.

Garth stopped cutting paper and looked at me. "Thanks, Humphrey," he said. "You gave me an idea of where to hide it!"

"You're welcome," I squeaked. "But I want to know what the treasure *is*."

"BOING!" Og said.

As Garth began writing on the squares of paper, I thought about treasures. In the books Mrs. Brisbane read to us in class, people often looked for treasure. It was always something special, like gold and silver coins. Or sparkly jewels.

Sometimes treasure was buried in the ground. Sometimes it was at the bottom of the sea.

I scurried to the side of my cage near Og's tank. "What kind of treasure would you like?" I asked him.

Og just stared at me with his goofy eyes. I didn't think coins or jewels would be of much use to a frog. He'd probably rather have crickets or flies. *Ewww.*

Coins or jewels wouldn't be of use to a hamster, either. But I still wanted to go on the treasure hunt.

Suddenly, a small voice called out, "Ham!"

Garth's little brother, Andy,

raced into the room. He came over to my cage.

"He's a hamster, not a ham," Garth told him.

"Ham!" Andy shouted.

I don't like being called a "ham." But Andy is very young, so it's okay.

Andy pointed at the squares of paper. "What's that?"

"That's where I'm writing down clues for the treasure hunt," Garth explained.

"What's that?" Andy asked.

"It's a game where my friends

have to follow clues and see who can find the treasure first," Garth said.

"What's that?" Andy asked, pointing at Og.

"That's Og the Frog," Garth said. "Now be quiet so I can think of the clues."

Garth put his finger to his lips and said, "Shhh!"

Andy put his finger to his lips and said, "Shhh!" Then he said, "Frog."

Andy stared hard at Og.

Og stared right back.

"BOING!" Og said in his funny voice.

"Shhh!" Andy said.

Og leaped into the water with a huge splash.

Garth sighed. "Mom!" he called. "Can you get Andy out of here? He's bothering me."

Garth's mom appeared at the door. "Let Andy help. He wants to be included in the party."

"I can't come up with clues with him around," Garth complained.

"You can only stay if you watch quietly," Garth's mom told Andy.

She put her
finger to her
lips and said,
"Shhh."

"Okay, I'll watch," the little boy answered. "Shhh!"

At first, Andy stood quietly as Garth wrote on the slips of paper.

"What rhymes with flower?" Garth asked.

"BOING!" Og said.

Poor Og. Doesn't he know that BOING doesn't rhyme with flower at all?

"Shower! That works," Garth said.

I was trying to think of a flower

that showered when Andy asked, "What's that?"

"A clue," Garth told him. "Like a riddle."

"Widdle," Andy said.

Aha! A clue is like a riddle! I like riddles. I was really curious about these clues.

Garth wrote some more. Then he asked me, "What do you think of this clue? 'Everyone knows you must water a flower. Tip me over. I'll give it a shower,'" he read.

"It's GREAT-GREAT-GREAT!" I

squeaked. But I had no idea what the answer to the riddle was.

As Garth wrote, he muttered other strange words, like "frown," and "goal," and "basket."

Then he opened a desk drawer and pulled out a treasure chest. It was so small, he could hold it in the palm of his hand. Still, it looked like a real treasure chest. It even had a tiny lock.

"What's that?" Andy said.

"It's the treasure for the treasure hunt. It's something

anyone in Room Twenty-six would love to have," Garth said.

Anyone? Even a hamster?

"Remember, this is a secret," he added. "Do you promise not to tell anyone?"

"Promise," Andy said.

"Promise," I squeaked.

"BOING!" Og agreed.

To my surprise, Garth opened the door to my cage!

Then he carefully put the treasure chest inside, covering it with my bedding. "Leave it right

there, Humphrey," he said. "And don't peek."

"Okay," I promised.

But even as I said it, I knew it would be a very hard promise to keep.

The Trouble
Begins

"A.J.'s here," Garth's dad called from the hallway.

Garth quickly hid all of the pieces of paper in his desk drawer. "He's spending the night," he explained. "But don't tell him about the treasure hunt."

"Okay," Andy said. "Shhh!"

A.J. raced into the room. "Hi, Humphrey Dumpty," he said.

He calls me Humphrey Dumpty for fun. I call him Lower-Your-Voice-A.J. because of his loud voice.

"Hi, Og," A.J. said.

Og answered with a friendly "BOING!"

"BOING-BOING!" Andy said.

Then he hopped across the room, shouting.

"Quiet, Andy," Garth told him.

A.J. leaned down close to Andy and said, "Shhh!"

Andy said, "Shhh!"

"Bedtime, Andy," Garth's dad called from the hallway.

Andy said, "Night-night, ham and frog."

The boys played a game. Then Garth's dad called from the hallway again.

"Time to wash up and get ready for bed, guys," he said. "You've got a big day tomorrow."

Once Garth and A.J. had left, I told Og, "We've got a big day tomorrow, too."

This time, Og was silent.

Maybe he wished the treasure was in his tank instead of my cage.

I wanted to open the treasure to see what was inside, but I'd promised Garth I wouldn't peek. It's always a good idea to keep a promise.

I hopped on my wheel so I wouldn't think about the treasure.

I was spinning FAST-FAST-FAST when the door to my cage started to open.

I wanted to see who was opening it, but my wheel was going too fast. I had to wait until it slowed down. While I waited, I saw the shadowy shape of a hand reach in and poke around the cage.

I had to see who was doing this, so I hopped off the wheel. I guess I hopped off too soon because I flipped head-over-paws across my bedding. When I stopped, I was dizzy.

The hand picked up the small treasure chest. I tried to see whose hand it was, but whoever it was must have been crouching down.

"Stop!" I squeaked as loudly as a small hamster can squeak. "Stop right now!"

"Shhh" was the only answer.

"Stop, thief!" I squeaked as my heart went THUMP-THUMP-THUMP.

No one answered. But I did smell something. Was it . . . chocolate?

"BOING-BOING!" Og called out as he splashed wildly in his tank.

Before I knew it, the hand took

the treasure chest out of my cage and closed the door. I dashed forward to see who it was, but it was too late. Garth's room was empty.

"Og, did you see the thief?" I asked.

Og didn't answer this time. I guess he hadn't seen who it was. Neither had I.

I couldn't believe it. The treasure chest was GONE-GONE-GONE!

~~~~~

When Garth and A.J. came back into the room, I squeaked up right away. "A thief was here!" I told them. "We have to find the thief!"

"Calm down, Humphrey Dumpty," A.J. said. "Shhh."

"Good night, Humphrey," Garth said.

He took off his glasses and got into his bed. A.J. got into the other bed in Garth's room.

"BOING-BOING!" Og said.

"Good night, Og," Garth said.

I love humans, but sometimes I wish they'd pay a little more attention.

The boys talked in the dark for a while. And soon I could

tell by their breathing that they were asleep. But *I* didn't sleep the whole night.

Like most hamsters, I am usually wide awake at night. But I'm not usually so WORRIED-WORRIED-WORRIED.

It had been nice to have the treasure chest in my cage. But it was not nice at all to have it missing!

I imagined what would happen the next day. One of my friends would be the first to reach my cage. But when that friend got there, they would not find the treasure!

I thought about how the winner would be disappointed.

Garth would be disappointed.

Garth's parents would be disappointed.

But nobody would be more disappointed than me.

~~~~~

The next morning, Garth jumped out of bed. I tried to tell him again the treasure was missing.

"You sound excited, Humphrey," he said while A.J. was out of the room. "So am I! And you're the most important guest, because you've got the treasure!"

Except, of course, I didn't.

He went downstairs to get ready for the party.

"I've got to do something, don't you think?" I asked Og.

"BOING-BOING-BOING!" he agreed.

Since the family was at home, I didn't dare go far from my

cage. I decided to search for a *new* treasure so the party wouldn't be ruined.

It's a secret, but I have a lock-that-doesn't-lock on my cage door. I can get in and out without any humans knowing it.

I jiggled the lock and the door opened. I was free!

It's a LONG-LONG-LONG way down to the floor for a small hamster, and I didn't have much time. So I decided to explore Garth's desktop first.

There was *a lot* to see on Garth's desktop.

The first thing I saw was a cup full of pencils. But these weren't plain pencils. They had amazing things on top, like an orange pumpkin head, a smiling monkey, and a shiny star. One

pencil looked like
a rocket ship!

Next to the pencil cup was a huge yellow smiling face. When I saw it, I smiled back.

"Hello," I said, trying to be friendly.

Then I saw that the smiling face was really a clock.

"Never mind!" I said.

Next to the clock was a frame made of twigs with a picture of Garth and A.J. in it.

I wandered around a deck of cards and ran right into a tiny pink pig. The pig fell over and let out an "Oink!"

"Sorry," I said. I quickly moved on.

There were pads of paper, a large blue feather and a pencil box with the planets on it. I know

about planets from our lessons in Room 26.

I kept on walking. Soon I was face-to-face with a row of tall dinosaurs with very large teeth. They weren't real dinosaurs, thank goodness. But they still were scary to a small hamster like me.

I scurried past a row of toy

cars in bright colors. One was a
bright red car with no top on it.
It was just my size and I stopped
to look at it.

I barely touched the shiny
car with my paw and it lurched
toward me.

"VROOOM!" the car roared.

"Eeek!" I squeaked. I started
running.

The car zipped across the desk, making wild turns. I ran for my life, zigzagging out of its way. Suddenly, I saw I was headed for the edge of the desk! It was a LONG-LONG-LONG

way down to the floor.

To my left was a pencil case that was taller than I am.

To my right was the *front* edge of the desk. Eeek!

At the last second, I leaped

up onto the pencil case. The car zoomed right off the edge of the desk. It sailed through the air and landed on Garth's soft bed.

"BOING-BOING!" Og said as I caught my breath.

My heart was pounding, but I told him, "Don't worry. I'm fine and so is the car!"

"BOING-BOING-BOING!" Og warned me.

He was right. I didn't have much time.

"I'll hurry," I told him.

Then something caught my

eye. Something shiny and gold, like treasure. It was a coin!

I hopped off the pencil case and scampered over to it. When I sniffed it, I realized that it wasn't a real coin. It was chocolate wrapped in gold paper.

Still, it was shiny and gold. And my friends all like chocolate.

I held it in my mouth, careful not to bite down and make teeth marks. I hurried back to my cage.

Og splashed loudly and called out, "BOING-BOING!"

And then I heard footsteps.

I dashed inside my cage and pulled the door closed behind me.

I slipped the chocolate coin under my bedding just as Garth came in.

"Time to go downstairs," Garth said. "The party's about to start."

The Hunt Is On

Garth and his dad carried my cage and Og's tank outside. They put us on a table under a large umbrella.

"A.J., could you come help me frost the cake?" Garth's mom asked. "You can lick the spoon."

"You bet!" A.J. replied.

Once he was gone, Garth said,

"We have to put the clues out
before he comes back."

Og and I watched
as Garth and his
dad put the little
squares of paper
around the yard.

They put them in odd places, like a watering can and a little red wagon.

"Hurry, Dad," Garth said.

Suddenly, I heard happy voices. My friends from Room 26 had arrived!

"Oh, Humphrey, I'm so glad you're here!" That was the voice of Miranda Golden. I think of her as Golden-Miranda because her hair is as golden as my fur.

"Hi, Humphrey! Hi, Og!" a giggly voice said. That had to be

Stop-Giggling-Gail. It was hard for her to stop giggling once she got started.

"HI-HI-HI!" I answered.

Once everyone had arrived, Garth's mom called the guests over to start a funny race. First, each of my friends stood in a sack. Then they had to hold on to the sack while they hopped to the finish line.

I wish Og could have tried that game. He's GREAT-GREAT-GREAT at hopping.

But Gail and her friend Heidi Hopper were good at hopping, too. They won the race.

Next, my friends split into pairs. Garth's parents tied one kid's right leg to the other kid's left leg. Then they had to work together to run to the finish line. It was FUNNY-FUNNY-FUNNY to see them try to run like that!

Seth and Tabitha won. They

are good friends who are both good at sports.

There were other games, too, but it was hard for me to enjoy them. All I could think about was the stolen treasure chest.

Finally, Garth announced that the hunt would begin. "There's *real treasure* for the first person who finds it," he explained.

That was true. It just wasn't the treasure Garth had planned on.

Garth read the first clue. "Everyone knows you must water a flower. Tip me over. I'll give it a shower."

My friends raced off in different directions.

"Og, I saw him put a clue in the watering can," I squeaked. "That must be it."

I was right. Mandy, Richie and Seth all raced to the watering can at the same time.

Mandy reached in and pulled out the next clue. She read: "The

sun is hot, as you will see. You'll be cooler under me."

Everyone squealed with excitement and raced to the umbrella over my table.

A.J. had to stand on a chair to reach the next clue. He read it out loud. "You'll find that you will never frown if you ride me up and down."

It took a little longer for my friends to figure out that riddle, but I quickly got it.

"The swing!" I squeaked.

They didn't understand me

right away. But soon they all
raced to the swing in the back of
the yard.

Tabitha grabbed the clue first
and read it. "If going places is
your goal, use me, for I am ready
to roll!"

"It's the car!" A.J. shouted.

Some of the kids raced toward

the driveway. But Heidi and Gail ran toward a little red wagon.

"That's it!" I shouted.

"BOING-BOING!" Og agreed.

Heidi reached into the wagon and pulled out the next clue. She read: "A-tisket, a-tasket. The last clue's in a basket."

I guess I wasn't paying attention when Garth and his dad hid that clue. I looked out at the yard.

I was confused. So were my friends.

A.J. and Richie ran toward a large plant in a basket. They

looked under all the branches but didn't find a clue.

Miranda hurried to Garth's bicycle. It had a wire basket on the front. But it was empty.

Seth and Tabitha ran to a basket of fruit on the food table. They searched and searched but there was no clue.

My friends all stopped and looked around the yard again.

Then Art spotted a tiny basket hanging from a low tree branch. He reached inside and found the clue.

"I got it!"
he yelled.

Then he read it. "You'll find the treasure—do not worry. Look for something cute and furry."

My heart went THUMP-THUMP-THUMP. This time *I* was the clue.

At first, my friends just stood

there. I could tell they were thinking hard.

A.J. picked up Andy's teddy bear from a chair. He looked and looked but there was no treasure.

"Cute and furry," I heard Miranda whisper to Sayeh.

Suddenly, Sayeh's face lit up. I call her Speak-Up-Sayeh because she's so quiet in class. But this time, her voice was loud and clear as she said, "Humphrey!"

Sayeh and Miranda raced to my cage. While Miranda looked on the outside of the cage, Sayeh

opened the door
and reached inside.

"Humphrey,   do
you mind if I look in
your cage?" she asked.

"Help yourself," I said.

She gently poked around in the bedding. "I found the treasure!" she called as she held up the candy coin.

Garth rushed to her side, looking VERY-VERY-VERY confused.

"That's not the treasure!"

he said.

Garth reached into the cage and poked around some more. Then he turned to face his friends. "The real treasure is missing," he said. "This is a fake treasure."

Sayeh looked confused.

Garth looked upset.

I was confused *and* upset. Most of all, I was sorry that everybody was so disappointed.

Mystery Solved

"**W**hat did you do with it, Humphrey?" Garth asked me. "Where did you hide it?"

"I didn't!" I squeaked. "A thief took it."

"Humphrey's just a hamster,"

Garth's dad said. "What could he do?"

"You don't know Humphrey," Garth said.

Some of my friends laughed. They knew I'd had a lot of amazing adventures.

"Humphrey wouldn't do anything bad," Miranda said.

"BOING!" Og added.

My other friends all agreed.

Garth nodded. "I know, but how could the real treasure disappear like that? And how did the chocolate coin get in Humphrey's cage?"

"I'm happy with the candy," Sayeh said. "Don't worry, Garth."

But Garth was still upset. "I know where that candy came from. It came from my desk."

"Do you think a thief came in and stole your treasure?" Garth's mom smiled. "And then replaced it with the candy? That's silly."

"No, it's not!" I squeaked.

"Somebody could have taken it while we were searching," Garth said. "We weren't looking at Humphrey's cage the whole time."

"True," Garth's dad said.

"False!" I said. "You're WRONG-WRONG-WRONG!"

Everybody laughed at my squeaking. I wish they'd at least try to understand me.

"I guess Humphrey knows what happened," Miranda said.

"He might be the only witness," Tabitha said.

She was almost right. Og and I were the only ones who knew that a thief stole the treasure the night before.

She didn't know that we had no idea who the thief was. I mean, who could it have been?

The only humans who were in

the house were A.J., Garth, his mom, his dad and Andy.

A.J. wasn't a thief. But had he been playing a joke on Garth?

Garth wouldn't have taken his own treasure. He wouldn't have wanted to ruin his own party.

Garth's mom and dad were too nice to steal anything. Plus, they

wouldn't want to ruin Garth's party, either.

And Andy had been asleep in bed when the treasure was stolen.

I looked at Garth's little brother. He didn't look like a thief. But he did look funny with chocolate smeared all over his face.

Garth's mom looked at him, too. "Andy! I told you no chocolate cake until later!" she said. "You sneaked some chocolate last night, too."

"Yum, chocolate," Andy said. "YUM! YUM! YUMMY," he sang.

Garth said, "Shhh!"

Andy said, "Shhh!" right back.

The thief had smelled like chocolate. Andy loved chocolate. And he'd been eating it last night.

The thief had said, "Shhh!"

Garth and A.J. said, "Shhh!" But Andy liked to say "Shhh!" a lot.

Andy had been in the house last night. But now I knew he hadn't been in bed.

I raced to the front of my cage. "You did it, Andy! You're the thief," I squeaked. "Turn yourself in!"

All my friends giggled at my SQUEAK-SQUEAK-SQUEAKs. But I didn't giggle.

"Andy is the thief!" I said. "He did it!"

"Humphrey seems mad at Andy," Garth said.

"Yes, he does," Garth's mom said. She turned to Andy. "Did you take the treasure out of Humphrey's cage?"

Andy looked down at the ground. "Yes," he said softly.

"Why?" Garth asked.

"I like treasure," Andy said.

Garth had another question. "And you put the chocolate coin in the cage?"

"I like chocolate," Andy said.

That wasn't a real answer, but Garth didn't notice.

"Go get the treasure," Garth's dad said. "*Now.*"

Andy went in the house. He came back out carrying the little treasure chest.

"Give it to Sayeh," Garth's mom

told him. "And tell her you're sorry."

Andy handed Sayeh the chest. "Sorry," he said. He looked REALLY-REALLY-REALLY sorry, too.

Everyone gathered around while Sayeh opened the tiny chest.

"Oh!" she said as she reached inside. "It's a gift card for Tilly's Toy Store!"

All my friends said, "Oooh."

Sayeh handed Andy the chocolate coin. "This is for you, Andy. Because you told the truth."

Andy smiled happily, until his mom took the coin to save for later.

"Thanks for solving the mystery for us, Humphrey," Garth's dad said. "You're quite a treasure yourself."

"BOING-BOING!" Og agreed.

Garth's dad laughed. "Og, you're a treasure, too."

Garth's mom announced it was time for cake and ice cream. All my friends ran off to the food table.

But Garth came right back. "Humphrey, I knew it wasn't you," he said. "You'd never steal anything."

He opened the door of my cage and stuck a small piece of carrot inside. "Here's a treat for you."

Yum! That lovely orange carrot was like sparkly treasure to me.

I hid it under the bedding in my cage for later on. I could have a treasure hunt all by myself.

"Thanks for making it a great party," Garth said.

"You're welcome," I replied. "It was a GREAT-GREAT-GREAT party."

And I meant it.

Look for the next
Humphrey chapter book

Humphrey's

Pet Show Panic